PRINCE OF THE STABLE

For my Dad, who has cleaned his share of stables. - C.R.

Printed in the United States of America.   ISBN 0-8167-4022-4

10 9 8 7 6 5 4 3 2 1

PRINCE OF THE STABLE

A HUNGARIAN LEGEND

RETOLD BY CHRISTOPHER KEANE   ILLUSTRATED BY CHARLES REASONER

TROLL

In the center of the world, in the middle of a kingdom, along the muddy bank of the Duna River, there lived a poor Magyar peasant and his wife.

The peasant worked very hard cleaning the king's stables every day. And with the single copper coin he earned each month, his wife bought just enough thread to patch their clothes, and just enough turnips to keep them from starving. Not even a fly got fat from the crumbs off their plates.

Yet the husband and wife were happy because they had a beautiful son named Andras. His dark curls and black pearl eyes were admired throughout the land, and the son soon became known as "Handsome Andras." The villagers said, "With those good looks, Andras, you should be a prince."

"Naturally," Andras agreed. "I should indeed be a prince."

All day long Andras would lie on his bed dreaming of castles. But each night his father would tromp into the shack in filthy clothes, smelling like the stables that he cleaned during the day.

"How is my Handsome Andras today?" his father would roar happily.

"Ugh," Andras would say, holding his nose. "Papa, please, I'm trying to breathe."

hen Andras became a young man, he told his parents, "I must leave you so that I may find my fortune."

"But we need your help with the work," said his father.

"No, Papa," said Andras. "I'm tired of raggedy clothes and the taste of turnips and, especially, the smell of the stables. I should be a prince."

His parents were very sad, but they wished only the best for their son. Taking a satchel of food, Andras said good-bye and left in search of his fortune.

For many days, Andras wandered across the land. Then, one morning, Andras stopped suddenly as a huge magpie with an emerald tail landed at his feet. He was quite startled when the bird spoke.

"I have a message for you," the magpie said, and it dropped a note from its beak.

Andras unfolded the note and read:

> *Dear Handsome Andras,*
> *I have a great desire for someone like you. Just follow*
> *my magpie and it will lead you to my castle. I hold*
> *my breath awaiting your arrival.*
>
> *Rozsa*
> *The Princess*

"At last, a princess for a handsome prince!" said Andras to the bird. "I shall hurry to her."

For months and months, Andras followed the magpie as it flew above him. Stopping only to rest and to eat, he traveled through oak forests and over tall mountains. His toes soon poked through the leather of his shoes. His clothes hung like dirty rags. And his beard grew and grew until he had to wrap it around his waist to keep from tripping over it.

Finally the magpie landed near a magnificent castle. Andras washed his face in a nearby stream and trimmed his beard with a sharp stone before he entered the castle.

In the middle of the great room on a golden throne sat Princess Rozsa. Andras thought she was the loveliest woman he had ever seen. It was easier to stare at the sun than to gaze upon her beauty.

Standing proudly, he announced, "My dear Princess Rozsa. Here stands your Handsome Andras. I have come at your request."

"Ah! You are here," said the princess, rising from her throne. Andras stood tall as the princess approached him.

She looked him over carefully. "Yes," she said. "I think you are perfect—just what I need."

Feeling his handsome looks spoke for themselves, Andras only nodded.

The princess beckoned him with a wave of her hand. "Come, Handsome Andras, let me show you to your place." Andras followed her through a doorway.

They entered a large room lined in silver with velvety carpets so soft and deep, Andras sank up to his ankles. Andras, admiring the riches, thought that this room was certainly made for a prince. But aloud, he asked, "Could this be for me?"

Princess Rozsa laughed and said, "Oh, no. This would not be suitable for someone like you, Handsome Andras."

Through another door they entered a larger room with walls of solid gold and carpets so soft and plush, Andras seemed to sink up to his knees. He asked, "Could this be for me?"

Princess Rozsa laughed sweetly and said, "Oh, no. This would not be suitable for someone like you."

Then they entered a room as large as a city, encrusted in diamonds, with carpets so soft, Andras felt as though he was wading through clouds. Now, here is a room worthy of a handsome prince, he thought, and he said, "Princess Rozsa, is this room for me?"

The princess again answered, "Oh, no, this wouldn't be suitable for you, Andras."

hey then walked through a door that led them out of the castle and to the royal stables. As the stable doors opened, Andras nearly fainted from the horrible smell. Horse dung covered the floors, and the poor horses wallowed in filth, flies buzzing all around them.

Covering her nose with her handkerchief, Princess Rozsa said, "As you can see, we have indeed held our breath awaiting your arrival. But I'm certain you will have the stables tidy and the horses groomed in no time at all."

Andras, thinking this a mistake, asked, "Me? You wish me to clean stables?"

The princess didn't seem to hear him. She continued, "I realize it's a big job, so you needn't bother cleaning that old nag in the corner. Just clean the stalls of my three royal horses, and keep them curried and groomed. For good work, you will be fed. For poor work, you will go hungry. And after one year, you may choose the hand of anyone in the kingdom."

"Except," she added, looking down her nose at him, "my hand shall never be held by a peasant."

Andras could only stare in disbelief as the princess turned and left him standing knee-deep in muck.

He stomped in the mud and kicked at the stalls, then sat in a corner to sulk. He wanted to run away, but since he had watched only the magpie during his journey, he didn't know the way home.

"Princes don't clean stables," Andras grumbled.

However, his empty stomach soon grumbled, too. Andras knew that if he wanted supper, he must work.

So work he did. Day after day, he shoveled and raked and scooped and scrubbed until his hands were coated with grime and the dirt was piled so thick in his hair that he could have grown radishes there.

At first he cleaned only the three royal horses. But he soon felt sorry for the lonely old nag in the corner stall. So he scrubbed and curried that horse until its coat gleamed like the others. He came to enjoy the silky feel of its clean coat against his cheek. At night, Andras slept in the corner stall, where the old horse's breath kept him warm.

Each week, Princess Rozsa came to the stables and praised him for his hard work. But Andras, ashamed of his appearance, lowered his eyes and said nothing.

O ne night, three days before the end of his year's work, Andras slumped into his stall. "What an idiot I've been," he sobbed. Then he covered his face with his hands and cried.

"Pardon me, young man, why are you crying?"

Andras jumped at the sound of a strange voice. He looked up and saw the old nag staring at him.

"Did you speak to me?" he asked the horse.

"Yes. The horses here are magical. I am Taltos. Now, tell me, why are you crying?"

Sniffling, Andras answered, "Because I thought I was so handsome that the Princess Rozsa would make me her prince. But now my clothes are rags, my hair is filthy, and I am only a prince of the dung heap."

"True," said Taltos. "But if I may say so, you are an excellent prince of the dung heap. After all, you have cared well for me when no others would. So if you wish to win the attention of the fair Rozsa, I will help you. Here is what you must do."

Old Taltos leaned down and whispered in Andras's ear.

The next morning, after Princess Rozsa rode off to the town fair, Andras doused himself with water from the horses' trough. Then Taltos drew in a huge breath and blew a hot blast of air out over him. Andras was instantly clean. His hair shined and his hands were scrubbed.

Next Andras reached into Taltos's feed bucket and pulled out a chestnut. Cracking open the chestnut, he discovered garments studded with diamonds. Quickly he put them on.

Climbing onto Taltos, Andras found himself astride a magnificent steed. The horse leaped into the air while Andras clung tightly to his flowing mane. Soon Taltos glided down to the fairgrounds, where he pranced for all to see. Andras looked magnificent in his radiant clothes. No one recognized him as the dirty stable boy.

Princess Rozsa noticed this mysterious stranger and hastened to meet him. As they rode and talked, she said, "You seem familiar, but never have I met a man as handsome as you." The young man bowed to her, smiled, and then quickly excused himself.

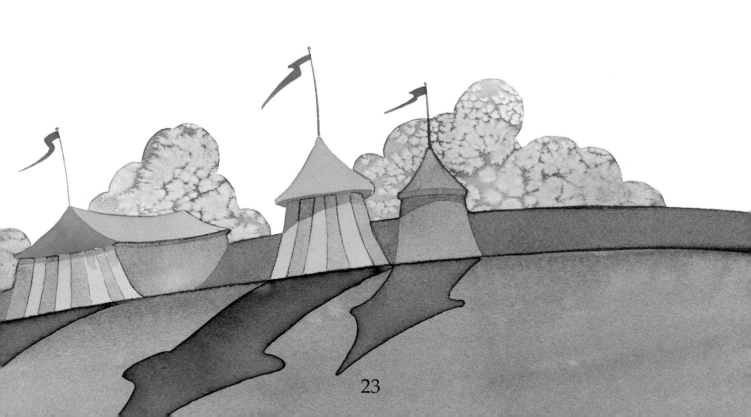

As fast as a thought, Taltos flew Andras to the stables. He took off the diamond-studded clothes, put on his rags, and smeared his face and hands with dirt.

The Princess returned to the castle and went to the stables. There was Andras, hard at work, streaming with sweat and clad in filthy rags.

"Have you seen a handsome prince ride by today?" asked Princess Rozsa. But Andras only lowered his head and said nothing. When Princess Rozsa saw he would not speak, she went away sadly.

he next day, Andras again donned his diamond-covered clothes. Again he appeared at the fair like an exotic prince. Princess Rozsa was so glad to see him that she spoke with no one else while they rode together. But after a short time, he again excused himself and vanished.

"Find him," the princess cried. "I must find my prince."

The princess raced back to the stable to question Andras again, but he only lowered his eyes and would not say a word. Princess Rozsa left with tears in her eyes.

On the third day, everything happened as before. When the princess rode forward to greet the mysterious prince, she told him he was the most wonderful man she had ever met.

This time, the princess had given orders that her attendants should hold tightly to the reins of the prince's horse so he could not get away. But Taltos was too powerful, and after a few minutes, Andras and his horse slipped from their grasp and vanished like a shooting star.

Andras quickly returned to the stable. He knew the princess would ride as fast as she could to try to catch him. There was no time to remove his splendid garments, so he threw his tattered clothes over them.

When Princess Rozsa arrived at the stable, she immediately noticed the diamonds shining through the holes in Andras's rags.

"It's you! You are my mysterious prince," exclaimed Princess Rozsa. "Why have you hidden from me?"

Andras removed the rags and wiped the dirt from his hands and face. He said, "Because I am only a poor peasant."

"Andras, in your diamond clothes, you are truly a handsome prince," said Princess Rozsa, smiling. "And now that your year of work is complete, you may choose anyone in the kingdom as your companion."

"Anyone?" asked Andras.

"Anyone," said Rozsa, and she held out her hand.

"Then I choose my good friend Taltos," said Andras. He leaped onto the magical horse and soared into the sky. He returned to his village, where he sold the diamonds from his clothes and built a castle for his parents. And forever after, Andras happily cleaned and cared for his horses, especially Taltos.

Russia

Eastern Europe

France

Hungary

Italy

Spain

The Prince of the Stable is a legend from Hungary. The Hungarian people, or Magyars, migrated from the plains in Eastern Europe and settled along the majestic Danube River. Hungary is a republic now, but for many centuries it was controlled by a few wealthy kings who ruled over the poor peasants.

The Magyar peasants, exhausted after each day's hard work, relaxed before bedtime by listening to folktales. In flickering candlelight, master storytellers told stories about enchanted kingdoms, treasure seekers, and magic animals. The legends often described the great differences between rich kings and their poor subjects. In those days, the Magyars said, "The pearl is not for the pig." They meant that a peasant could never be a king.

The story of Andras is an example of a heroic quest. During his quest, Andras is befriended by a horse called *Taltos*, which means "sorcerer" in Magyar. The Taltos horse is a common figure in Hungarian legends. Its magic is always used to help the hero. Taltos helps Andras learn that kindness and hard work are more important than beauty and wealth.

Magical helpers like Taltos are found in legends throughout the world. For example, many people will find a similarity between Taltos and the Fairy Godmother in the familiar story of *Cinderella*.